PUFFIN BOOKS

Unicorn School

First Class Friends

Willow started to back up when a
strong wind seemed to blow up
from nowhere. It swept into her,
knocking her off her feet.
'Willow!' she heard Sapphire gasp
from behind her.
The wind swept Willow straight
towards the edge of the cliff.
'Help!' she whinnied in alarm.

Linda Chapman lives in Leicestershire with her family and two Bernese mountain dogs. She used to be a stage manager in the theatre. When she is not writing she spends her time looking after her two young daughters, horse riding and teaching drama. You can find out more about Linda on her website lindachapman.co.uk or visit mysecretunicorn.co.uk

Books by Linda Chapman

BRIGHT LIGHTS
CENTRE STAGE

MY SECRET UNICORN series

NOT QUITE A MERMAID series

STARDUST series

UNICORN SCHOOL series
(*Titles in reading order*)
FIRST CLASS FRIENDS
THE SURPRISE PARTY

First Class Friends

Linda Chapman
Illustrated by Ann Kronheimer

PUFFIN

PUFFIN BOOKS

Published by the Penguin Group
Penguin Books Ltd, 80 Strand, London WC2R ORL, England
Penguin Group (USA) Inc., 375 Hudson Street, New York, New York 10014, USA
Penguin Group (Canada), 90 Eglinton Avenue East, Suite 700, Toronto, Ontario, Canada M4P 2Y3
(a division of Pearson Penguin Canada Inc.)
Penguin Ireland, 25 St Stephen's Green, Dublin 2, Ireland (a division of Penguin Books Ltd)
Penguin Group (Australia), 250 Camberwell Road, Camberwell, Victoria 3124, Australia
(a division of Pearson Australia Group Pty Ltd)
Penguin Books India Pvt Ltd, 11 Community Centre, Panchsheel Park,
New Delhi – 110 017, India
Penguin Group (NZ), 67 Apollo Drive, Rosedale, North Shore 0632, New Zealand
(a division of Pearson New Zealand Ltd)
Penguin Books (South Africa) (Pty) Ltd, 24 Sturdee Avenue, Rosebank,
Johannesburg 2196, South Africa

Penguin Books Ltd, Registered Offices: 80 Strand, London WC2R ORL, England

puffinbooks.com

First published 2007
2

Text copyright © Working Partners Ltd, 2007
Illustrations copyright © Ann Kronheimer, 2007
All rights reserved

The moral right of the author and illustrator has been asserted

Set in Bembo
Typeset by Palimpsest Book Production Limited, Grangemouth, Stirlingshire
Made and printed in England by Clays Ltd, St Ives plc

British Library Cataloguing in Publication Data
A CIP catalogue record for this book is available from the British Library

ISBN: 978-0-141-32247-6

To Charlotte, Beatrix and Damaris Ambery

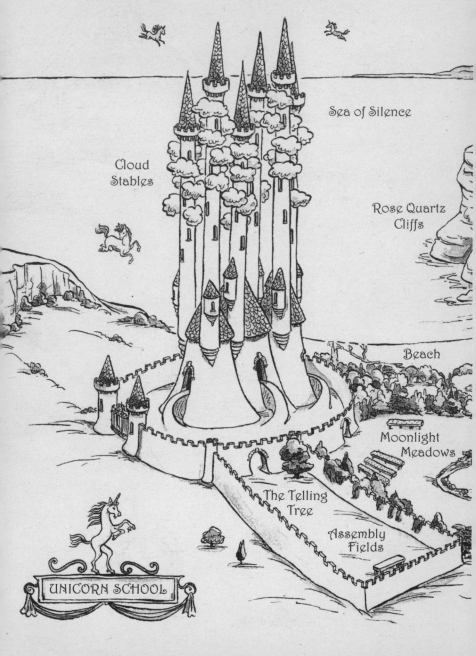

Arcadia

Sea of Silence

Cloud
Stables

Rose Quartz
Cliffs

Beach

Moonlight
Meadows

The Telling
Tree

Assembly
Fields

UNICORN SCHOOL

High Winds Pass

Bramble Forest

Flying Heath

Charm Fields

N
W · E
S

Contents

Chapter One

Unicorn School

'Are we nearly there?' Willow, the small snow-white unicorn, whinnied eagerly as she and her parents cantered across a meadow of lush green grass in Arcadia.

Willow's mum, a beautiful light grey unicorn called Stardust, nodded. 'It's just round the next corner.'

Willow plunged forward in excitement.

'There's no rush, Willow!' her dad called. 'The gates won't be open yet.'

With an impatient snort, Willow slowed to a trot. She couldn't wait to get to Unicorn School! All the young unicorns in Arcadia went to boarding school when they were nine. At school they learnt how to fly properly and how to use their horns to do magic things like casting charms, healing wounds and seeing into the future. *It's going to be great fun*, Willow thought.

She and her parents trotted up a hill. As they reached the top, Willow stopped dead and stared. The school and its grounds were spread out in the valley below.

'Oh, wow!' Willow breathed.

Unicorn School was an enormous castle with big golden gates and several pointed turrets. Its pearly-white walls glimmered and purple flowers with gold spots on their petals dotted the grass around it. Five tall elves with pointed ears were standing in front of the golden gates. They were wearing sparkling silver uniforms. Unicorns swooped down from the sky, their horns glittering and their long manes and tails swirling around them.

Willow watched in awe as the flying unicorns landed effortlessly on

the grass. Some of them only looked
about eleven or twelve and yet they
flew so confidently. She wished she
could do it as well as them.

'Well, what do you think?' her dad
asked.

'It's brilliant!' Willow exclaimed,
looking at the castle and at the
unicorns who were cantering up to

each other and talking about the summer holidays. They all seemed so much bigger than her. Willow knew that she was small for her age – something her annoying older brothers usually teased her about.

'I wonder which of these unicorns are Year Ones like you,' her mum said as they trotted down the hill towards the golden gates. 'And who you'll make friends with.'

Willow glanced around at all the other unicorns. She felt strangely shy. Usually she liked meeting other unicorns but everyone else seemed to know each other and have friends to talk to.

Her dark eyes fell on a big white

unicorn nearby. He was standing with a unicorn who looked as if he might be his father. They had the same silvery-white horns, handsome straight noses and thick dark grey manes.

I bet he's a Year Three at least, Willow thought, looking at the tall unicorn. She watched the way he was standing close by his dad's side and frowned. It was strange he looked nervous and he didn't seem to be talking to anyone like the other older unicorns were.

The unicorn's father bent his head. 'I'll leave you now, Storm,' Willow heard him say. He glanced at the gates. The elves had started to bustle about, taking out registers. 'It looks like the gates are about to open. Have a wonderful first term here.'

'Thanks, Dad!' Storm, the big unicorn, snorted.

Willow frowned. First term! So he must be a Year One unicorn like her. But he looked so much older. Her mum nudged her. 'We should go, Willow. The elves need to organize everyone into their houses.'

'Houses?' Willow said, wondering what her mum meant.

'All the unicorn pupils belong to a house – Star House, Moon House, Rainbow House or Sun House,' her mum explained. 'You'll eat with the people in your house and share a stable with them too.'

'And later in the term there will be competitions between the houses,' her dad added.

'I wonder which house I'll be in,' Willow said.

'Well, your brothers were in Rainbow House when they were at school, so maybe you will be too,'

her mum answered. 'Now goodbye and be good.'

'Course I will be!' Willow replied.

Her dad chuckled. 'That'll be a first!'

'Dad!' Willow stamped a hoof crossly.

Her dad snorted softly. 'You know I'm only joking. I'm sure you'll make us proud of you.' He touched his horn to Willow's neck. She felt a tingle of magic flowing through her then her nervousness faded.

She lifted her head and her dark eyes glowed. 'I *will* make you proud of me,' she told them strongly. 'I promise I will.'

Her mum smiled. 'Goodbye,

Willow!' Both Willow's parents touched horns with her and then they took off into the air. Willow watched them swoop away until they became small dots in the blue sky. Now that her parents had gone, she suddenly felt very alone.

Three older unicorns walked past her. They looked about eleven. The one leading the group had dark grey legs and black eyes that sparkled mischievously. He nudged his friends. 'Look at that teeny-tiny Year One.'

One of his friends – a girl – smiled at Willow. 'Isn't she cute?'

'I'm not cute!' Willow said, tossing her head. She didn't like being called teeny-tiny or cute. She was nine after all!

The leader of the group walked up to her. 'Are you missing your mummy and daddy?' he whinnied teasingly.

'No,' Willow replied. She was, but there was no way she was going to admit it to the older unicorn.

He looked at her for a moment. He reminded her of her brother Cassius. He had the same teasing gleam in his eyes.

'Didn't you know,' he said to her, 'Year Ones always go into school first?' He glanced at the shut gates. The elves were standing in front of them talking. 'You just go up to the gates and bang on them three times with your horn and then the elves will let you in.' He stared at her with wide innocent eyes.

But Willow wasn't fooled. 'Really? I think you missed out the bit about me having to turn a somersault first.' She laughed and swished her tail. 'As if I'm really going to do that. I'm not stupid!'

The unicorn's friends giggled and he looked slightly taken aback. But then he gave an easy shrug. 'OK, maybe you're not!' he said, grinning back at her.

'Come on, Oriel,' the girl unicorn said. 'Let's go and find the others!'

The older unicorns cantered off.

They swerved round a crowd of
very grown-up-looking unicorns
who looked like Year Sixes.

'Slow down there!' one of the
elves called out. 'No cantering in
front of the gates!'

Oriel and his friends ignored him.
Oriel put his head down and gave a
cheeky buck. The elf's face turned

red with rage. 'Why . . . you . . . you . . .'

Just then, one of the other elves stepped forward and blew a long note on a bronze horn. He was wearing a green velvet hat with three corners and looked like he was the elf in charge. As the horn's note floated out, the unicorns all stopped talking. When everyone was silent the elf cleared his throat.

'Right, everyone, it is time to go into school. Can you all line up in your houses please?' The other four elves stood in a line beside him. 'Star House, Sun House, Moon House and Rainbow House,' the chief elf said, pointing to each of the elves in turn. 'Year Ones, you will find out your houses when you go in, so I would like you to line up in front of me!' He took a list of names out of his pocket and unrolled it.

The unicorns moved into five separate lines. Willow trotted forward and found herself near the front of the group of first years. Oriel and his friends were jostling each other in the line for Rainbow House. The elf in charge looked like he was getting very cross with them. Willow turned round and saw Storm joining the line of Year Ones.

'Oh, for goodness sake!' The elf in charge of Rainbow House bustled over. 'What are you doing?' he said very crossly, pointing at Storm. 'You're not a Year One. You're far too big. Now get out of that line right now!'

Willow saw Storm look embarrassed. 'But . . . but I *am* in Year One,' he said, his voice little more than a whisper.

The elf glared at him. 'Don't be ridiculous! Of course you're not! Now which house do you belong to?'

Storm looked very anxious. People were staring at him curiously. 'I . . . I don't know. This is my first term,' he stammered.

'Right, that's it!' the elf exclaimed.

'I've had enough of this! Out of this line! You're going straight to the Headmaster!'

Chapter Two

Making Friends

Oriel and his friends sniggered. Storm looked as if he wanted to sink into the ground. Willow couldn't bear it. 'He *is* in Year One!' she exclaimed, stepping out of line. She was aware of everyone turning to look but she didn't care. 'I heard him saying goodbye to his dad,' she told the elf. 'It *is* his first term here!'

The elf frowned and for a horrible moment Willow thought he was about to tell her off too. Then suddenly another unicorn walked out of the line to stand at her side.

'It's true,' a voice said timidly. 'I heard him saying goodbye to his father too.' Willow glanced round. The unicorn who had spoken was very pretty, with a silver mane that swept almost to the floor and large dark eyes fringed by thick eyelashes.

Storm looked at them both gratefully.

Just then, the chief elf walked up to him with a list. 'What's your name?'

'Storm,' the tall unicorn replied.

The chief elf checked his list and nodded. 'I have a Storm listed here as being a new Year One. It appears you *are* in the correct line.'

'I'm sorry,' the elf in charge of Rainbow House said to Storm. 'You are so tall I thought you must be a

Year Three playing tricks.' Everyone
continued to stare at Storm until
the chief elf blew a long note
on the horn. Two of the elves
opened the golden gates.

'Year One unicorns follow me!'
the chief elf announced.

He marched through the gates.

Storm fell into line beside
Willow and the other unicorn
who had spoken up for him.
'Thank you,' he said to them as
the elf led them through the gates
and across a grassy courtyard.
'People always think I'm older than
I am. I'm Storm. What are your
names?'

'Willow,' Willow replied.

'And I'm Sapphire,' the pretty
unicorn said shyly.

They all smiled at each other.

'It's weird actually being here, isn't
it?' Storm said. 'At school, I mean.'

Willow knew what he meant.
She'd thought about coming to
school so much, it was very strange

to finally be there — and to know she wouldn't see her mum and dad again for ages.

'I wish my brothers and sisters were here,' Sapphire whickered nervously. 'I'm not used to doing stuff without them.'

'How many brothers and sisters have you got?' Willow asked her.

'Six,' Sapphire replied. 'Two of them are older than me and four of them are younger.'

'Wow, I've just got two brothers and that's enough!' Willow said.

'And I haven't got any brothers or sisters at all,' Storm put in. 'I can't imagine having six of them! It must be very noisy!'

'It is.' Sapphire looked wistful. 'I'm really going to miss them.'

'Do you think we'll all be in the same house?' Willow asked eagerly. She might have only just met Storm and Sapphire but already she felt that she would really like to be friends with them.

'Looks like we're about to find out!' Storm replied as they followed the elf through an archway in the courtyard into a large walled field. At one end there was a table with a stone top. An old, very noble-looking unicorn was standing behind it. His body was snow-white without even a speck of darker grey. Willow stared. Most unicorns had horns that were gold, bronze or silver, but this unicorn's horn was striped in all three colours.

'That must be the Tricorn,' Willow whispered. She looked at him in awe. Her brothers had told her the Tricorn was the school's Headmaster and knew more about magic than any unicorn in Arcadia.

'Quiet, please!' the chief elf commanded. He organized the Year Ones into a line in front of the Tricorn. The rest of the school trooped into the field and lined up behind them.

When all the unicorns were still the Tricorn stepped forward.

'Welcome!' he said, his strong voice ringing out round the field.

Hardly a unicorn moved. The Tricorn's gaze swept over the Year Ones. 'You will gain much from being at school, but you must be prepared to listen and learn.' His eyes seemed to linger on each one. They all stood very still. 'First, you must start by learning your houses.' He stepped forward and touched his horn to the stone table. Willow saw it glow and a list of names appear on it in four columns of swirly writing.

'Please step out as I call your name,' the Tricorn said. 'In Rainbow House: Starlight, Topaz, Willow . . .'

Willow's heart leapt and she stepped forward. *Oh, please let Storm and Sapphire be in Rainbow House too,* she thought.

'Sapphire . . .'

Willow exchanged delighted looks with Sapphire.

'Flint, Ash, Troy . . .'

Willow glanced round. Storm was looking worried.

'Storm,' the Tricorn finished.

Willow felt a rush of relief as Storm joined her and Sapphire. She gave him a friendly nudge with her head and Sapphire nuzzled him. He looked really pleased.

The unicorn called Troy, who was also in Rainbow House, edged closer to them. 'Hi,' he said. He was short and muscular and held his head proudly.

'Hi,' they all whispered back and smiled.

The Tricorn read out the names of the Year One unicorns in the other three houses. 'And now it is time to go and find your stables,' he announced. He lifted his head so his stripy horn glinted. 'School dismissed!'

Four older unicorns trotted up to the Year Ones.

'I'm Juniper,' said one, a handsome dappled-grey unicorn with strands of black running through his mane and tail. 'We're Year Sixes, and we're going to show you the stable where you'll sleep and then give you a tour of the school. Will the Year Ones in Rainbow House please follow me?'

Willow and the other Year Ones in Rainbow House walked towards him.

Juniper smiled round at them. 'Come on! I'll take you all up to your stable!'

Chapter Three

Watch Out!

The eight Year Ones in Rainbow House followed Juniper out of the walled field into one of the towers. A corridor wound its way upward. 'The stable where you'll be sleeping is at the top of the tower,' Juniper told them. 'It takes a while to reach it walking up this way, but when you've learnt to fly it'll be much quicker.'

'Will we all be together?' Sapphire asked Juniper.

He nodded. 'There are eight stalls in each stable, one for each of you.' He trotted along until they reached a round room with large windows and a door in the wall opposite.

'We're in the clouds!' Sapphire exclaimed, looking out of the large windows.

Ash, one of the other unicorns, looked round in surprise. 'Where's the stable for sleeping?'

'In the clouds,' Juniper said with a smile. He touched his glittering

horn to the door in the wall, and it
swung open. On the other side was
a white fluffy cloud. It had a short
tunnel running through the centre
of it. At the far end was a large
room split into eight stalls separated
by low walls. Windows had been
carved out of the cloud walls, and
each stall had a bucket of fresh
water and a large net of hay.

'That's your stable,' Juniper told

them. 'The second years are on the cloud above you; the third years above them. It's the same all the way up, with the sixth years being on the highest cloud at the top.'

'Wow!' Willow stepped into the cloud tunnel. The floor felt soft and bouncy under her hooves. She touched the walls of the tunnel with her nose as she walked through it. A wisp of cloud floated away like a piece of cotton wool. There were silver name plaques hanging over the entrance to each stall. Troy was in the stall at the end on the right. Next to him was Storm, then Willow, and then Sapphire next to her. On the other side of Sapphire

was Topaz, then Starlight, Flint and
Ash.

The Year Ones went into their
stalls. The cloud on the floor was
even softer and fluffier. Willow
giggled. 'I can't wait to go to bed
tonight!'

'This is cool!' Storm snorted.

'Do you want to look round the
rest of the school now?' Juniper
asked.

'Yes, please!' they all replied eagerly.

They followed Juniper back down the tower to the ground. 'You've already seen the Assembly Fields,' Juniper said, pointing with his horn towards the fields where the Tricorn had spoken to them. 'And through here,' he pointed at a nearby archway, 'are the Moonlight Meadows.'

He led the way through the archway. A large meadow was spread out in front of them. It had a glittering stream and shady trees around the edges. There were lots of unicorns in it talking and grazing and flying. 'This is where we eat and also where we come between lessons,' Juniper said.

The school was huge. Juniper took them through the Charm Fields – where they would learn about charms – to the Sea of Silence, a still, silvery sea that edged on to a white sandy beach. Juniper pointed with his horn to the pinky-grey cliffs that rose up where the beach ended. 'Those are the Rose Quartz Cliffs where you'll learn how to use your magic to see what's happening anywhere else in Arcadia.' He cantered along the sand and up a steep path. There was a vast area of short grass and tangled bramble bushes at the cliff top.

'This is the Flying Heath,' Juniper
explained.

'What's that forest over there
called?' Willow asked, pointing with
her horn at a thick forest of tall
trees that edged the Flying Heath.

'That's Bramble Forest,' Juniper
answered. 'We go through it to get
to High Winds Pass where we
sometimes play sports and have

races. Come on. I'll show you.'

The forest was thick and deep. The trees towered overhead.

'High Winds Pass is up here,' Juniper said, turning off the main track and leading the way up a narrow twisting path. 'Year Ones are only allowed to go there with a Year Six or a teacher. It's very easy to get lost on the way.'

They took several more turnings, all the time going higher and higher. Willow could see what Juniper meant about it being easy to get lost! She was sure she'd *never* be able to remember the way up there on her own.

At last the path ended and they

stepped out of the trees. The top of the mountain was a large flat area of ground with a steep drop all around it. The unicorns' manes swirled around them as they stood on the short grass.

'It's very windy!' Starlight said, sheltering beside Juniper.

'It looks a great place for having races, though!' said Troy, looking at the perfectly flat area of grass.

'It is fine in the summer when the winds drop,' Juniper replied.

Willow cantered to the edge of the grassy area and looked down the mountain. Storm trotted after her. The sides were rocky and steep.

'Be careful!' Juniper whinnied.

'Sometimes there can be really
strong gusts of winds up here. Don't
stand too close to the edge, Willow.'

Willow started to back up when a
strong wind seemed to blow up
from nowhere. It swept into her,
knocking her off her feet.

'Willow!' she heard Sapphire gasp
from behind her.

The wind swept Willow straight
towards the edge of the cliff.

'Help!' she whinnied in alarm.

Chapter Four

Storm to the Rescue

Willow thought she was about to be swept over the cliff but the next second there was a flash of white and Storm plunged in front of her, placing his body between her and the cliff edge. Willow knocked into him. She fell to her knees.

'Are you OK?' he whinnied.

'Yes!' Willow scrambled to her feet as Juniper came cantering over.

'Willow!' Juniper exclaimed anxiously. 'I thought you were going to fall over the cliff!'

'So did I.' Willow's legs were

trembling with shock. If she'd been swept over the cliff edge she would have been killed! She swung round to Storm. 'Thank you,' she said shakily.

'You could have got knocked over yourself, Storm,' Troy whinnied. 'You were very brave to do that!'

Storm looked pleased but a bit embarrassed.

'Come on,' Juniper said worriedly. 'If the winds have started coming in gusts like that then it's too dangerous to stay here. We'd better go back. And just remember, no coming up here on your own,' he warned them all.

'We won't,' Willow said fervently. There was no way she ever wanted to go up to High Winds Pass again!

Juniper led them back down through the forest. As they reached the Moonlight Meadows, they heard the sound of a horn blowing. 'It's almost lunchtime,' Juniper told them.

An army of elves appeared, carrying silver buckets of food each with a unicorn's name on. They put them on to five long tables that had round holes in for the buckets. 'This is our table,' Juniper said, showing the Year Ones to the Rainbow House table. 'The teachers eat there,' he added, pointing to a table where some adult unicorns were already eating. He nodded to a tall, muscular unicorn with kind eyes.

'That's the Head of Rainbow
House. He's called Atlas and he
teaches flying. You'll meet him later.'
Willow found her bucket of food
and plunged her nose in. Delicious!
Bran, boiled barley and oats. Her
favourite! Storm was next to her
and Sapphire and Troy were
opposite. Juniper joined the table
next to Troy.

As they all began to eat, Willow saw Oriel, the teasing unicorn from Year Three, further up the table. When his eyes fell on Storm and Willow he grinned.

'Hey, it's Little and Large,' he called out.

Willow smiled. She and Storm probably did look quite funny together. After all, she only came up to his shoulder. She glanced at Storm who looked uncomfortable. 'Just ignore him. Oriel's only teasing,' she said.

'Were you stretched when you were a foal?' Oriel called to Storm. 'Or did your parents plant your hooves in fertilizer to make you grow?'

The other Year Threes sniggered. Storm hung his head.

'Oriel!' Juniper said sharply. 'Stop teasing Storm or I'll report you to Atlas!'

'All right. Don't get your horn in a twist, Juniper,' Oriel said cheekily, but he turned back to his food and stopped teasing Storm.

'So, when do our lessons start?'
Troy asked Juniper.

'This afternoon,' Juniper replied. 'I
checked your timetable and after
lunch you've got a magic charms
lesson followed by a flying lesson.'

Willow's ears pricked. Wow!
Charms and flying! She couldn't wait!

After lunch, Juniper took the Year
Ones in Rainbow House to join the
other Year One unicorns in the
Charm Fields.

'Enjoy your lesson,' he told them.

'Thanks,' they all chorused.

The charms teacher was a very
slim unicorn with pale-grey dapples
and a tail that swept all the way to

the floor. She smiled round at them with friendly eyes. 'Hello, everyone. My name is Damaris and I will be teaching you about charms and curses. As I'm sure you all know, a charm is something that helps you or brings you good luck and a curse is something that does something bad to you.'

The unicorns all nodded.

'You can charm or curse an object so if a unicorn wears the object or sleeps with it for a night they will be affected by it,' Damaris continued. 'Curses are contagious, which means that you can catch them simply by touching another unicorn who has the curse.'

Troy lifted his head to raise his horn. 'Why do we have to learn about charms and curses? My father's always told me that unicorns shouldn't use magic like that; unicorns should use the magic inside them.'

'Your father is completely right,' Damaris replied. 'But occasionally it is useful to know how to charm something, in case you need to help someone who you can't be near enough to touch with your horn.' She fixed the class with a stern look. 'Unicorns of course should *never* use curses. We only teach you about them so you know how to avoid them. Now today I'm going to teach you how to make a good luck charm. Let's begin.'

Damaris gave each of the unicorns an old metal horseshoe, and explained how to cast a good luck charm by touching it with their horns and imagining all sorts of lucky things. She told them that when the horseshoe was properly charmed it would turn silver and glitter.

It was hard to do, but by the end of the lesson most of the unicorns had managed to make their horseshoes glitter a bit. Willow's horseshoe was one of the shiniest. 'Well done,' Damaris praised her as she collected the horseshoes. 'It looks like you might be a natural at this.'

Willow glowed with happiness. She liked being good at magic!

'Why can't we just do magic?' Storm asked. 'Why do we need lessons? I've read that unicorns who live in the human world can do proper magic as soon as they first turn into their magical unicorn shape. Why can't we be like that?'

'A very good question, Storm,' Damaris answered. 'The secret unicorns who live with humans are born with a lot of magic, so they don't have to practise in the same way as we do.' Damaris smiled. 'However, one day I'm sure you'll all find it just as easy to do magic as the secret unicorns do.'

Willow exchanged looks with Sapphire. She hoped so!

After the lesson, Damaris took them up the cliff path to the Flying Heath to meet Atlas for their first flying lesson.

The teacher began by organizing them into a line. 'Flying isn't difficult so long as you are prepared to practise,' he told them. 'Soon you'll find it as easy as cantering. By the end of this term you should be able to play games in the sky and have flying races. The important thing to remember is that you must believe you can do it, and when you get up in the air just take things very slowly. No racing round until you can turn and land. Do you understand?'

They all nodded.

He made them practise taking off, flying a little way up in the air and then coming back down. 'The mistake unicorns always make is to fly too high before they're ready and then they start crashing into things and losing control.'

I can do this, Willow told herself. She took a deep breath. *Fly*, she thought. A shiver of magic ran across her white coat, her body seemed to get lighter and then suddenly she was rising into the sky rather rapidly.

Down, she thought quickly as she remembered what Atlas had said about not flying too high to start with.

She floated down to the ground. As she landed lightly she gave a pleased whinny. All around her, unicorns were rising up into the air and landing again. Troy was really good at it. He

was going very high up then coming
down and landing perfectly. But no
one seemed to be having problems –
well, apart from Storm, Willow
realized. He seemed to be finding it
hard to get off the ground.

'You have to believe you can do it,'
Atlas told him. 'Try harder and give a
little push with your back legs.'

A look of determination crossed
Storm's face. He pushed down hard

with his strong back legs and flew upward into the air. 'Whoa!' he cried, his legs flailing. Several other unicorns had to land hastily to get out of his way.

'Come back down!' Atlas called to him.

But Storm didn't seem able to control himself. He shot backwards.

Troy was just behind him. 'Stop!' he shouted in alarm.

In an effort to avoid Troy, Storm tried to plunge forward and shot straight into Sapphire! She spun round out of control. Her legs kicked but she couldn't save herself. With an alarmed whinny, she crashed down on to the ground.

No Good at
Flying

'Sapphire!' Willow whinnied.
Storm landed on his knees.
He scrambled up and cantered over
to Sapphire, who was lying on the
ground.

Atlas reached her at the same time.
'Are you all right?' he demanded.

The heavy landing had knocked

all the breath out of Sapphire. She
gasped for air. Atlas touched his
horn to her chest. His horn glowed
and a second later a look of relief
crossed Sapphire's face as Atlas's
magic began to work and her
breathing slowed.

Next, Atlas touched his horn to a
long scrape on her side. It healed
over instantly.

'Oh, Sapphire, I'm sorry I bumped

into you!' Storm exclaimed wretchedly. 'I'm so big and clumsy.'

'It's OK,' Sapphire told him as she got to her feet and shook the dust from her coat. 'It was just an accident.'

'I'm so stupid,' Storm groaned.

'No, you're not,' Atlas told him kindly. 'You just need to learn how to use your strength properly. But you'll get better the more you practise.'

'I'll help you, Storm,' Troy offered. 'We can practise in between lessons.'

Atlas looked round at the others. 'Come on then, everyone, the excitement's over. Let's try again.'

★

By the end of the lesson, everyone apart from Storm was able to fly a few metres into the air and then land without crashing. But Storm wouldn't go more than a few centimetres off the ground. He seemed very worried about hurting someone again.

When the lesson finished it was time for tea. As they all headed back to Moonlight Meadows, Oriel came cantering by. He grinned at Storm. 'I just heard about your flying lesson. It sounds like you had a *smashing* time.' He sniggered at his own joke. 'You have to be the clumsiest unicorn ever, Storm!'

Storm looked very awkward.

Willow glared at Oriel. 'No he's not!'

'Well, just so long as I'm not flying when he is!' Oriel replied. 'I don't want to be bulldozed into the ground!' He laughed and cantered off.

Sapphire nuzzled Storm. 'Ignore him.'

Troy looked crossly after Oriel.

'Don't worry. I'm sure you'll be great at flying soon.'

But Storm didn't look convinced.

The next week raced by. There was so much for them all to learn – more flying and charms and curses, rose-quartz gazing and healing, unicorn history lessons and lessons about the geography of Arcadia and the human world. Willow, Sapphire, Troy and Storm became good friends. They had great fun together. But Storm was still having problems learning to fly. Whenever he flew more than a little way off the ground he seemed to panic. To make it worse, the other Year One unicorns were all improving quickly. By the end of the week, Willow and Sapphire could turn and circle in the air and Troy could dive and swoop like a Year Three. They could all fly up to their stable in the clouds, but they never did because they didn't want Storm to feel left out.

On Friday, when everyone was getting ready for a flying lesson, Storm hung back. 'Are you coming?' Willow asked him.

'I've got a sore back,' Storm replied, avoiding her eyes. 'Atlas said to rest in my stall.'

'Can't you get Atlas or one of the other teachers to heal it?' Sapphire asked in surprise.

'Unicorn healing magic should
only be used for serious injuries. I
just need to rest it,' Storm whinnied.
'See you later!' He hurried away.

'He doesn't look like he's got a
sore back,' Troy said suspiciously.

'I think he's making it up to get
out of the flying lesson,' Willow
declared.

'Poor Storm,' Sapphire snorted.
'He's really unhappy that he can't
fly.'

'He's not going to get better if he doesn't come to lessons.' Willow frowned in the direction of the stables. 'We should tell him he's got to come and practise.'

'Atlas will be really cross if we're late,' said Troy, looking worried.

'I know,' Willow whinnied. 'But I think we should talk to Storm. Look, why don't you two go on and say I'm on my way?' The others nodded and she set off for the stables.

When she reached the courtyard she stopped in surprise. Storm was standing on the far side, talking to another unicorn. It was Oriel!

Why was Storm talking to Oriel? Willow wondered. *Usually all Oriel ever did was tease Storm and make him feel uncomfortable.* Their backs were towards her. She edged closer and saw Oriel pass Storm something. She couldn't see what it was but Storm took it in his mouth.

Oriel cantered off.

Storm turned and saw Willow. He looked very guilty.

'What did Oriel just give you?' Willow demanded, trotting over to him.

'Mind your own business!' Storm mumbled. And before Willow could say anything more he cantered away swiftly towards the stables.

The Silver
Horseshoe

'Wait, Storm!' Willow whinnied. She cantered after him but Storm was much faster than her. By the time she reached the top of the tower, Storm was already standing in his stall. There was nothing in his mouth, but Willow spotted a small heap of cloud at his feet.

Willow was panting for breath.
'What are you hiding?'

'I don't know what you're talking
about,' Storm muttered.

Willow looked at the lump on the
ground. 'So what's that you're
covering up then?'

'Nothing,' Storm said hastily. 'No!
Wait!' he exclaimed as Willow
stepped forward and impatiently

swept away the cloud with one of her front hooves.

A glittering silver horseshoe lay on the floor.

'OK,' Willow said slowly, looking up at Storm. 'What's going on?'

Storm sighed. 'It's a lucky charm,' he admitted unhappily. 'Oriel told me that if I sleep with it in my stall tonight then it will help me fly better tomorrow.'

Willow was puzzled. 'You know we're not supposed to use charms to help with our magic. But why would you trust anything Oriel gave you?'

'He came to say sorry for teasing me about my flying. He was really nice,' Storm said. 'He said he wanted to make up for the teasing by helping me.'

Willow blinked. 'Maybe he isn't so bad after all,' she said. 'But you still mustn't use the charm, Storm. It would be really wrong.'

Storm looked longingly at the glittering horseshoe. 'Perhaps if I just used it once, I'd learn what to do and then be able to fly without it.' His voice dropped. 'You don't know what it's like being so bad at flying, Willow,' he snorted unhappily.

He looked so sad that Willow couldn't help feeling sorry for him. 'Well,' she said slowly, 'maybe using it just once won't matter too much.

But after that you must *promise* to go back to flying using your own magic.'

Storm nodded. 'I will. I promise.'

Willow realized how late she was for the flying lesson. 'Look, I'd better go,' she said.

'Please don't tell the others,' Storm begged her. 'They'll just laugh at me.'

'They won't,' Willow said. 'But if you really don't want me to tell them I won't.'

'Thank you!' Storm said.

And leaving him looking much happier, Willow cantered down the tower.

Luckily Atlas was late for the flying lesson too. With a rush of

relief, Willow joined Sapphire and
Troy.

'Is Storm OK?' Sapphire asked
anxiously.

Willow nodded. She longed to tell
Sapphire and Troy about the charm
but she had to keep her promise to
Storm. 'He's fine. He's going to
come flying tomorrow.' She had an

uncomfortable feeling in her tummy. What was going to happen then?

At breakfast next day Storm was looking happy and excited. 'You seem in a good mood,' Sapphire said to him.

Storm nodded. 'I can't wait to go flying today.'

Sapphire and Troy looked astonished.

Willow gulped. She was beginning to have a seriously bad feeling about this. The more she thought about it, the more strange it seemed that Oriel would have given Storm a lucky charm. Further along the table, she saw Oriel and his three friends Sorrel, Gemini and Hera watching them. Oriel whispered something and his friends all giggled. Willow's feelings of unease grew.

After breakfast all the Year Ones made their way to the Flying Heath. 'Today you're going to concentrate on changing speed when you're in the air,' Atlas told them. 'You need to learn how to go from slow to fast and then back to slow again.'

Willow slipped into place beside Storm. 'Good luck,' she whispered.

'Thanks.' He smiled at her anxious face. 'Don't worry, Willow. I can tell this is going to work. I feel great today!'

Atlas told them to take off. Willow felt her body sparkle with magic and pushed down with her back legs. She plunged into the sky. She loved flying! She wondered where Storm was and glanced round.

Storm was cantering up into the air. He looked confident and happy, but then all of a sudden his body began to flip over.

'Whoa!' he cried as he ended upside down. The next minute he was spinning round and round in the sky.

He crashed into Flint who whinnied in alarm and then gasped as he started spinning round too. 'Help! Atlas! I can't stop turning!'

Flint whinnied. He spun into Moondust, a Year One from Star House, and she started turning too.

'What's going on?' she neighed.

Atlas galloped into the sky as Storm crashed into Topaz and Starlight, setting them spinning as well. 'Come down!' But as he spoke, Flint bumped into him and the next second Atlas was spinning round too!

Within seconds, the sky was full of spinning, whinnying unicorns!

Willow hastily dived to the ground, avoiding the other unicorns. She suddenly realized what was happening. The horseshoe that Oriel had given Storm wasn't a good luck charm. It was cursed!

'Help!' Sapphire gasped from above.

Willow was the only unicorn not spinning — well, apart from another group of older unicorns who were having their lesson at the far end of the heath. She galloped towards them. She had to get help!

As she got nearer she saw that the unicorns were third years. Oriel and his friends were hanging around

near the outside of the group, watching the chaos among the Year Ones and laughing so hard they could hardly stand. Willow glared at them furiously. How could Oriel have done something like that to Storm! But right now she didn't have time to stop. She raced up to the teacher, a tall skinny unicorn called Fabian. He was busy instructing a group of third years in diving techniques and hadn't noticed the commotion at the other end of the heath.

'Help!' Willow gasped, skidding to a stop beside him. 'My class has caught a curse! Please help!'

Oriel's Dare

As soon as Fabian realized what was happening, he plunged into the sky, his golden horn glittering. He flew to the other end of the heath and touched each of the spinning unicorns with his horn, muttering a short spell as he did so. One by one, the unicorns stopped spinning. Looking very dazed, they all flew down to the ground.

'Thank you,' Atlas whinnied gratefully to Fabian. He looked round sternly at the Year Ones. 'Who was responsible for this curse? Someone could have crashed into the ground and been seriously hurt!'

No one said anything.

'Well?' Atlas demanded.

Storm stepped forward. 'It . . . it was my fault,' he admitted.

Atlas looked very surprised. 'You? But why, Storm? Did you think it was going to be funny?'

'No,' Storm stammered. 'I didn't mean it to happen. Honestly. It was just . . . ' He hesitated. 'Well,

someone gave me a charmed
horseshoe. I thought it would help
me fly. But it must have been
cursed, not charmed after all.' He
hung his head in shame.

'Storm! You should know better
than to try and improve your flying
through charms!' Atlas snapped
angrily. 'Who gave you the
horseshoe?'

Storm didn't answer.

Willow glanced round at the Year Threes. She saw Oriel looking guilty. He slipped to the back of his class.

'Storm, if you don't tell me you will go back to your cloud stable and stay there for the rest of the day. And there will be no sports all week!'

Storm looked upset but he still didn't tell Atlas who had given him the charm.

'Very well,' Atlas said coldly. 'Go to your stable now. I'll be up to see you after the lesson has finished!' Storm walked unhappily away.

Willow felt awful. It wasn't fair that he was getting into trouble because of Oriel!

'Right, everyone, back to the lesson,' Atlas said. 'I think we'll do some talking on the ground while you all recover. And I hope the rest of you have learnt a lesson — never to use charms to help you in your flying!'

At break time, Sapphire and Troy joined Willow. 'What are we going to do?' Sapphire said worriedly as they watched Atlas heading towards the cloud stables. 'Storm will be in such trouble if he doesn't tell Atlas who gave him the horseshoe!'

'I don't understand,' Troy frowned. 'Who would have done something so mean?'

'I'll give you one guess.' Willow glanced at Oriel who was walking across the heath towards the school, sniggering with his friends. Hot anger flashed through her. Oriel wasn't at all upset that he'd got Storm into trouble. Not caring that they were Year Threes and much bigger than she was, she trotted over to them and glared at Oriel.

'You think you're so funny, don't you?' she said.

Oriel grinned. 'Yes, actually, I do.'

Sapphire and Troy joined Willow as she stamped one of her front hooves furiously. 'You've got Storm into real trouble!' she told Oriel.

The older unicorn shrugged. 'It's his fault for being so stupid. He shouldn't have taken the horseshoe.'

'He's not stupid!' Willow exclaimed. 'You're mean. You shouldn't have done it!'

'Ooh,' Oriel teased. 'Is he your boyfriend?' His friends sniggered.

Willow was too angry to care. 'Well, I think you should own up. Storm is getting into even more trouble now because he won't say who gave him the horseshoe.'

Oriel looked at her as if she was mad. 'I'm not owning up. *I'd* get into trouble then.'

Willow felt like hitting him with her horn. 'But it's *your* fault.'

A sly gleam suddenly came into Oriel's eyes. 'All right. I'll tell you what. I've got an idea.' He motioned with his head for Willow to walk away from the group with him.

She followed the older unicorn very warily. What was he up to?

'I'll own up,' Oriel said, much to Willow's surprise. 'But on one condition.'

'What?' Willow said suspiciously.

'That you come with me to High Winds Pass and stand in the middle of it all on your own.'

'High Winds Pass?' Willow faltered.

'Are you chicken?' Oriel smirked at her. 'I heard you were so frightened when you went there on the first day that you couldn't even stand up.'

'That's not true!' Willow said hotly. 'I was knocked over by the wind!'

'Well then, if you're not scared, you'll do it.' Oriel looked at her challengingly. 'I dare you!'

Willow didn't know what to say. She didn't want to go there and she didn't trust Oriel. But if it would help Storm . . .

'All right,' she said slowly. 'But you've *got* to own up afterwards.'

Oriel nodded. 'OK. Let's go after lunch. I'll meet you here. Don't tell anyone!' And with a laughing whinny he cantered back to his friends.

Troy and Sapphire questioned Willow all lunchtime about what Oriel had said to her, but she refused to tell them. She didn't want them to come with her and maybe get into trouble too. After lunch, she pretended she was going up to the cloud stables, but instead of heading to the courtyard she cantered to the heath. She felt sick. She really didn't want to go up to High Winds Pass with Oriel.

Oriel was waiting. 'Ready? Or have you changed your mind?'

Willow didn't want him to see that she was afraid. 'Of course not,' she replied scornfully, hoping her voice wasn't trembling too much. 'Let's go!'

They cantered into the forest. Oriel led the way through the trees and up the twisting, turning path to the top of the mountain. As they got closer to the top Willow could hear the wind whistling through the trees. A shiver ran through her as she remembered almost being blown over the edge of the cliff. She wished they could go back. *I'm doing this for Storm*, she reminded herself.

She raised her voice over the wind. 'Where do I have to go?' she whinnied to Oriel.

'Just out on to the mountain top,' Oriel snorted. 'Stand in the middle for the count of ten and then the dare's done.' He slowed down as they reached the top of the path.

'Go on. I'll wait for you here!'

Willow cantered out on to the flat mountain top. The wind was swirling around. She was almost blown off her feet. But she forced herself to the centre of the pass and counted to ten. 'Done it!' she cried, looking round for Oriel.

But there was no sign of him.

'Oriel!' Willow whinnied.

There was no reply. Struggling against the wind, Willow made her way back to the path. Where had Oriel gone? There was no sign of him anywhere. 'Oriel!' she whinnied again.

Oriel poked his head out from round a tree near a bend further down the path. 'Tricked you! Now let's see if you can find your way back to school on your own!' He turned and with a flick of his tail galloped away!

'No!' Willow neighed. There was no way she could find her way back without Oriel. 'Come back!'

A faint laughing whinny floated up the path but Oriel didn't come back. She was on her own. The wind blew even more strongly.

Fear gripped Willow. She stepped towards the path. A gust of wind buffeted against her, throwing her down to her knees. She staggered up and was almost knocked over again by an even stronger gust.

CREAK!

A nearby oak tree bent in the wind. An ear-splitting cracking noise came from its trunk.

Willow leapt back as the oak tree was ripped from the ground.

It crashed to one side with a splintering, cracking noise. Leaves and twigs flew into the air across the path. Willow's heart pounded. She could have been killed! Her mane whipped around her as she walked towards the oak tree. It had fallen straight across the narrow path and was blocking her way down the mountain. There was no way she could get past it! It was far too big for her to jump over and she'd never be able to fly in this wind. She tried to push her way through the trees on either side of the path, but there were so many brambles and thorny bushes that she just got tangled up. She pulled backwards, tugging her mane free. She couldn't get over the tree trunk and she couldn't go round it. How would she ever get back to school?

The wind howled around her. Panic gripped her. She was trapped!

Chapter Eight

Trapped!

Willow's sharp eyes caught a flash of white on the other side of the tree.

'Oriel!' she gasped as he cantered up to the tree trunk.

Oriel looked shocked. 'What happened?'

'The tree blew down,' Willow

whinnied above the howling of the wind. 'Why did you gallop off like that?'

Oriel looked very guilty as he peered at her though the tree's branches. 'I just meant to give you a fright. I thought it would be a good trick to play. I was going to come back. I wasn't going to leave you here.'

'But now I'm trapped!' Willow exclaimed. 'How can I get out from here?'

'I don't know,' replied Oriel. He tried pushing the tree with his shoulders but it was much too big for him to move. 'I'll have to get help!'

Willow felt panicky. What would the teachers do when they found her there? All of the Year One unicorns knew they weren't allowed up to High Winds Pass on their own. Maybe she'd be expelled.

As if he could read her thoughts, Oriel spoke quickly. 'I won't tell the teachers. I'll ask my friends to help. Will you be all right while I go back to school?'

Willow nodded bravely. 'But be as fast as you can!'

'I will. See you soon!' And with that, Oriel galloped off.

It was horrible waiting for Oriel to come back. Willow paced up and

down beside the tree trunk. Oh, why had she come there? She just wanted to be safe at school with her friends. Tears pricked her eyes. What if the teachers *did* find out and she was sent home? What would her parents say? And what about Sapphire and Troy and Storm? She'd never see them again if she had to leave.

Be brave, she told herself.

She took a deep breath and tried to gather her courage. She concentrated hard on Sapphire, Troy and Storm. Oh, if only they were with her!

It seemed like ages, but eventually she heard the sound of whinnies on the path. She raced to the tree trunk. Above the roaring of the wind she could hear the sound of hooves. Suddenly Oriel and three other unicorns came galloping up the path.

Willow stared. Oriel didn't have his friends with him. He had Sapphire, Troy and Storm instead!

They raced up to the tree.

'Willow!' they all whinnied.

'Oriel told us what happened,' Troy exclaimed as he screeched to a stop. 'He told us about bringing you up here as a joke . . . '

'And about the tree blocking the path,' Sapphire gasped.

'None of *my* friends would believe me,' Oriel said unhappily. 'They just thought I was trying to trick them.'

'We hadn't seen you for ages,' Storm said. 'We were sure what Oriel said must be true. Especially when he told us you'd come here to try and help me.' He nuzzled Willow through the tree's branches. 'We're going to rescue you!'

'Stand back!' Oriel told her. 'And we'll try to move the tree trunk.' He, Storm, Sapphire and Troy began to push the tree with their chests. It moved a few centimetres and then stopped.

'It's too heavy!' Oriel panted.

'Give me more room!' Storm said.

They made a bigger space and Storm placed his strong shoulders

against the trunk. 'All together!' he whinnied.

Willow watched anxiously.

'Push!' Storm exclaimed.

Storm's muscles strained and he stepped forward step by slow step, pushing the tree out of the way until there was just enough space for Willow to squeeze through.

'Hurray!' she exclaimed as she squeezed through the gap and plunged on to the path.

The other unicorns broke off pushing and whinnied in delight.

Willow nuzzled Storm. 'Thank you, Storm!'

'I didn't do anything much,' Storm said, with a shy grin.

We couldn't have done it without you,' Oriel told him. 'It's lucky you're so big and strong.'

'You were great, Storm,' Willow said.

'Yes,' Sapphire said, stepping forward. 'But we'd better get back before the teachers realize we're missing.'

As they galloped into the trees, Oriel said, 'It'll be quicker if we fly back.'

'But . . . but I can't fly,' Storm stammered.

Willow looked at his frightened face. 'I bet you can. You were amazing just now when you moved the tree.'

Storm hesitated.

'Have a try, Storm,' Sapphire urged him.

'Yes, go on,' said Troy.

'I bet you *can* do it,' Oriel told him.

A spark of confidence flared in Storm's eyes as he looked round at them all. 'All right,' he said bravely. 'I'll try!'

They lined up. 'OK. One, two, three!' Oriel said.

Storm pushed down with his back legs and took off beside Willow. 'You're flying!' she whinnied as they rose into the sky.

'I am!' Storm gasped, wobbling beside her. He looked down and for a dreadful moment Willow thought he was going to panic. She touched him with her horn. 'You can do it,' she whispered.

His eyes met hers. 'Yes,' he said determinedly. 'I can!'

They flew side by side down the mountain. Swooping out of the woods they flew across the heath. They landed and galloped into the Moonlight Meadows.

Oriel's friends were grazing together. They looked up in astonishment as Oriel cantered into the meadows with Willow, Sapphire, Troy and Storm.

'So it was true,' Gemini said. 'You did need help.'

'We thought you were joking!'
Hera exclaimed.

'Well, I wasn't,' Oriel told them.
'Willow really was trapped behind a
fallen tree. But Storm managed to
move it. He was brilliant! He's so
strong!'

'It wasn't just me,' Storm said
modestly.

'No, but we couldn't have done it
without you,' Oriel told him.

'We'd have had to get a teacher if
you hadn't been there and then I'd
have got into so much trouble,' said
Willow. She threw Oriel a cross
look.

'I'm sorry, Willow,' he said. 'I
should never have dared you to go

to High Winds Pass. I wish I could
make it up to you.'

'Well . . .' Willow glanced towards
Storm. 'You could do what you
promised. That would be a start . . .'

Oriel nodded. 'All right.' He
looked Storm squarely in the face.
'I'm sorry about giving you the
cursed horseshoe, Storm,' he said. 'It
was a stupid trick. I'm going to tell
Atlas it was all my fault.'

'But you'll get into trouble,' Storm whinnied in alarm.

'I know, but it's not fair if you get into trouble instead of me,' Oriel told him. 'Thanks for not telling Atlas I gave you the horseshoe. That was really good of you.' He touched Storm's neck with his nose. 'I'm sorry I've been teasing you. It's great that you're so big. I bet you'll win all the flying races for Rainbow House at the next sports day.' He looked across the meadows to where Atlas was. 'See you later . . .' He grinned. '. . . If I survive the telling off that Atlas is probably going to give me!'

He cantered towards Atlas. Willow

iled. Maybe Oriel wasn't so bad
after all.

'Let's go and tell the others in
Rainbow House what's been
happening,' Gemini said. 'They
should know how brilliant Storm's
been.' Hera and Sorrel nodded and
the three of them trotted off.

'You'll be a hero when everyone
hears about this,' Troy told Storm.

'And just think, you can fly now!'
Willow exclaimed.

Storm's eyes lit up. 'You're right, I
can! I flew all the way down from
the mountain.'

Willow grinned. It was great
to see Storm looking so happy
at last.

'Now we can race in the sky,' told him.

'And fly up to our stables,' said Sapphire.

'I love being at Unicorn School!' Storm declared.

Willow looked round at her friends. She loved being at Unicorn School too. So much had happened in the few days since they'd arrived. She wondered how many more adventures they were going to have.

Lots, the little unicorn told herself with a smile.

Don't miss the next book in the

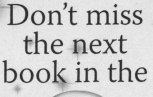

series!

Out now!

And watch out for
Unicorn School: The Treasure Hunt,
coming soon.

Also from Linda:

My Secret Unicorn:
Starry Skies

Stardust:
Magic Secrets

Not Quite a Mermaid

Linda Chapman

You don't need a tail to make a splash!

Electra is different from other mermaids.
She has legs instead of a tail and is always getting
into scrapes in search of adventure!

Electra's class is having a competition to collect magic mermaid
fire from the seabed – the deeper you dive, the more you can find.
Will Electra and Splash be brave enough to dive to the very bottom?

puffin.co.uk

My Secret Unicorn

When Lauren recites a secret spell, Twilight turns
into a beautiful unicorn with magical powers!
Together Lauren and Twilight learn how to use
their magic to help their friends.

Look out for more *My Secret Unicorn* adventures:

The Magic spell,
Dreams Come True, Flying High,
Starlight Surprise, Stronger Than Magic,
A Special Friend, A Winter Wish, A Touch of Magic,
Snowy Dreams, Twilight Magic

Puffin by Post

...corn School: First Class Friends – Linda Chapman

If you have enjoyed this book and want to read more,
then check out these other great Puffin titles.
You can order any of the following books direct with Puffin by Post:

Unicorn School: The Surprise Party • Linda Chapman • 9780141322483	£3.99
More magical fun with Willow and her friends	

My Secret Unicorn: The Magic Spell • Linda Chapman • 9780141313412	£4.99
Lauren's pony, Twilight, turns into a secret unicorn!	

My Secret Unicorn: Rising Star • Linda Chapman • 9780141321226	£4.99
A magical adventure with Lauren and Twilight.	

Not Quite a Mermaid: Mermaid Fire • Linda Chapman • 978014138370	£3.99
You don't need a tail to make a splash!	

Stardust: Magic by Moonlight • Linda Chapman • 9780141317793	£4.99
First in a series of fairy magic and adventure.	

Just contact:

Puffin Books, C/o Bookpost, PO Box 29,
Douglas, Isle of Man, IM99 1BQ
Credit cards accepted. For further details:
Telephone: 01624 677237
Fax: 01624 670923

You can email your orders to: bookshop@enterprise.net
Or order online at: www.bookpost.co.uk

Free delivery in the UK.
Overseas customers must add £2 per book.

Prices and availability are subject to change.

Visit puffin.co.uk to find out about the latest titles, read extracts and
exclusive author interviews, and enter exciting competitions.
You can also browse thousands of Puffin books online.